Pearl's Wisdom

Bethany Bare

Halo
PUBLISHING INTERNATIONAL

Halo Publishing International
7550 W IH-10 #800, PMB 2069,
San Antonio, TX 78229

First Edition, May 2025
ISBN: 978-1-63765-752-2
Library of Congress Control Number: 2025903461

Halo Publishing International is a self-publishing company that publishes adult fiction and non-fiction, children's literature, self-help, spiritual, and faith-based books. Do you have a book idea you would like us to consider publishing? Please visit www.halopublishing.com for more information.

Cameron, Winnie, Kazimira, and Kai,
May you share your inner wisdom with the world.

Foreword

Witnessing the elegant power of a musician and poet who picked up the brush has been a true gift. I remember when I first connected with Bethany and heard the way she understood deep in her bones the power of the Intentional Creative process; she began to use it as the tool it is. This precious offering of a book invites a sacred window into the soul of an artist's rebirth as herself.

~Shiloh Sophia McCloud
cofounder of MUSEA:
Center for Intentional Creativity®

PREFACE

Bethany Zare uses a painting technique called Intentional Creativity. The process allows for a conversation between the canvas and the artist. Bethany floats the paint and lets the muse lead the storytelling. Simply put, this process removes control from the critic (left side of the brain) and allows the muse (right side of the brain) artistic liberty and freedom to play.

When people don't understand the role of their inner critic, they either give it too much credence, which stifles creativity, or ignore it, which allows the critic to be in control. The most successful way of cohabitating with the inner critic is to accept it, welcome it, thank it for all it does, and reassure it that everything will be okay, especially if the muse is allowed to play.

Whether playing her horn, writing poetry, or painting, Bethany is aware of the symbiotic relationship of the muse and the critic housed in her DNA. By releasing old stories and wounds, she embraces a new perspective on life.

The story *Pearl's Wisdom* is told through the poetry accompanying the paintings. Each image started with an underlayer on the canvas, some of which are displayed. If you look closely, you may be able to see the original images underneath the final painting.

At the end of each poem, there is a pearl of wisdom. See if you can find them all.

CONTENTS

In a small village at the edge of the world, a child was born under a sky that hummed with cosmic energy. From the moment Pearl took her first breath, the world around her whispered in colors and shapes, inviting her to see beyond what was visible. Her heart was filled with a hunger to create and play.

Birth of an Artist

Finding the right frequency
to vibrate her soul,
ready for the journey
from baby's first cry,

Pearl enters this earth.
She arrives as a visitor with a body
and somehow stumbles
into her voice.

It's time to take center stage.
The curtain rises.
No dress rehearsal,
for life starts now.

WE ARE ALL DYING
FROM THE MOMENT OF BIRTH,
SO WHAT ARE YOU WAITING FOR?

As Pearl grew, she began to realize her gifts. She found she could talk to the animals and play music on her French horn.

LIMITING BELIEFS

The soul begins its journey as a sack of
brilliant stars awaiting launch. She bursts
from the womb with special powers unbeknownst to her.

Shamed for cheating, but she really could see
the future. She hid her gifts and sustained her
first wound.

You aren't believable.

She found her first love—the twisted brass tubes,
shiny and bright—in a clunky, heavy case.
She poured her heart and soul into that horn.

Innocence ended at fifteen when the teacher
acted on her schoolgirl crush and crushed her sense of self.
Resilient beyond belief, she packed her second wound.

Passion isn't safe.

Unprepared for the harshness of the world,
she was teased for being different.
This completed her bag of limiting beliefs.

You're not good enough.

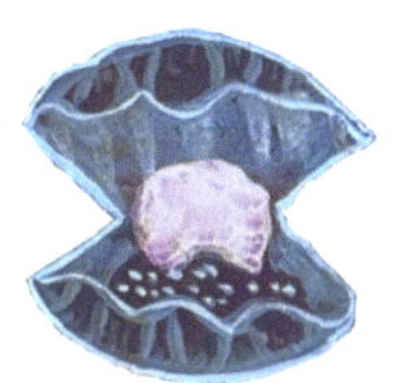

YOU ARE LOVABLE
EVEN WITH YOUR FLAWS.

Sometimes, she doubted herself because she was too different. The other children in the village didn't understand her. They laughed at her. "You talk to animals? You play the horn? That's weird!"

DAWN OF EMPOWERMENT

She arrived on earth with magic abilities,
talking with animals and other possibilities.
Many did not comprehend
why she was different and not like them.

Horn in hand, she practiced furiously.
Not good enough, she felt, curiously.
Searching for love and constantly fishing,
finding only that something was missing.

Affirmations didn't fill her soul.
She only felt a gaping hole.
Not knowing how to close the gap,
the opinions of others felt like a trap.

So quick to give away her value,
but it was she who needed rescue.
No longer worried how others viewed her,
she discarded what didn't serve her.

STOP LOOKING OUTSIDE
FOR ANSWERS THAT ARE INSIDE.

One night, Pearl was in her attic bedroom, looking out the window at the stars, when she found a spider near her bed. She felt more curious than scared and started a conversation.

Inkling of Consciousness

The invitation came to expand her perception beyond herself.
So Pearl contemplated the meaning of life.

What if that bug were me or I were it, she thought.
I wonder if it has any friends?

Finally, she asked out loud, "Who are you, and who am I?"
That's when she heard a small voice say, "I'm a being, just like you."

This startled her and filled her with many questions. She wanted to share
this newfound friend with her parents, so she ran downstairs, even though
it was after her bedtime.

"Why are you still up?" her father asked in a harsh tone.
"There's a bug in my room," she started to say, momentarily excited
to introduce him to her new friend.

Before she could explain, her father pounded up the stairs to the attic. She
trailed behind and heard a loud *thwack*.

All of her dreams and wonders about the world disappeared
with an audible gasp. "Now go to sleep," he said.

KEEP ASKING
HARD QUESTIONS.

One day while sitting in the garden, a small mouse scurried up to Pearl's feet and spoke in a gentle voice. "You must search beyond the ocean's depths, where the wind moves through the trees to find hidden pearls of wisdom," said the mouse. "Listen with your heart, not just your ears, and trust that the sound of your horn will lead you."

Message from a Mouse

Pearl had searched life's maze,
but no purpose felt redeeming
until she found a mouse who said,
"I'll help you find your meaning."

With no sign of what Pearl sought,
the mouse made a suggestion,
"Is it possible you're looking
in the wrong direction?

"You must follow the music
and readjust your frame.
Only self-reflection
will make you whole again.

"Stop the chatter and adjust your view.
Your purpose will become clear.
You must take a trip and collect wise pearls.
Play is the new frontier."

From that day forth, she understood
her mission to find the buried gems.
When she felt lost, she would seek more guidance
from her earthly furry friends.

WHAT IF YOUR TRUE LIFE
IS HIDDEN IN THE MAZE
OF THE CURRENT ONE?

The mouse's words filled her with both wonder and determination, as though she had just received a calling that she couldn't ignore. She gathered her horn, ready to understand the depths of her soul and begin the journey inward. This quest was the reason she had come to Earth.

YOUR INNER WILDERNESS

I beg you to explore
both inside and out
your source down to the pores
and seek what it's all about.

Don your Sherlock Holmes
and approach every mystery
with a fresh set of eyes
looking at your history.

Leave no stone unturned
lest you sound the alarm.
Each fire left unburned
can fester and cause harm.

From the time you were in utero,
you had a mission to discover.
Walk through the exotic inner wilderness
to find your internal lover.

Pearl rushed to the edge of the ocean and stared at the vast horizon. She set sail in a boat made just for her. The ocean spoke to her with every passing wave, "Each pearl holds a secret. You must dive into the depths of your heart to find the wisdom they carry."

IN SEARCH OF PEARL

She set sail from a place far away,
over the ocean and through the sea.
She rode from mystic shorelines through the fog,
with only the sound of her horn to guide her.

She followed her heart in search of pearls.
Shimmering at the bottom of the sea,
each little pearl she harvested would sustain her.

As the magical sounds left the horn,
some of the notes cracked
and fell off the staff into the safety of her hand,
for she was the pearl catcher.

All the missed notes returned to the ocean to create
wisdom from a million grains of sand.
The cycle of forgiveness for imperfection
continued throughout her quest.

LIFE ISN'T A SERIES
OF PERFORMANCES.
IT'S ABOUT THE JOURNEY.

Pearl arrived on a large beach and stepped off the boat onto the soft sand. She found a protected spot under the brilliant moon to rest for the night. Her dreams were filled with wild horses galloping towards her. They were free, untamed, and beautiful. As she watched them, she felt the stirrings of her own freedom, the call to embrace her wild, unshackled self. She knew she had to live her truth with the same unrestrained passion.

Dreams of Wild Horses

Ocean waves drag her
from murky dreams.
Consciousness escapes,
the world not as it seems.

Unsure, unclear,
can't quite awaken.
Is this real life,
or is she mistaken?

The midnight mane
of moonless night
welcomes her feet
in the sandy delight.

Listening now,
the sound of hooves.
Coming towards her,
horses running loose.

Pearl realized that she, too, could be free from the doubts that had held her back, free from the fear of being different. The dream filled her with a sense of purpose and strength. She was not just a girl with a horn; she was unstoppable, powerful, and ready to follow her true path.

The precise rhythm
matching that of the heart.
Enchantment and wonder
give her a start.

Painted ponies,
not one but many.
As she stands on the beach
encircled by plenty.

Salt in the air, horizon aglow
untamed spirits, a majestic sight.
They disperse with a jolt
by the edge of the night.

The comfort of horses
makes her succumb.
Back to sleep,
the sound of waves welcome.

WHAT'S HOLDING YOU BACK
FROM YOUR UNBRIDLED SELF?

In the middle of the night a muse appeared to give Pearl a gift. "Here is a magic paintbrush," the muse explained. "It will help you see the world in new ways and unlock the hidden truths around you. Don't hurry to find the answers. The pearls of wisdom you seek will reveal themselves when you are ready."

MOONLIT MUSE

Moved by whispers in the night,
a melody passes from ancient flight,
travels over moonlit pond,
across the veil from beyond.

A sound emanates from the whistling bird
as a vibrating heart can be heard.
Frogs awaken; their croak abounds,
adding to the symphony of sounds.

Until the muse connects the dots,
music and art, deep in her thoughts.
She hands over a magic painting brush
with an invitation not to rush.

Now's the time to use your tools,
painting insight with your muse.
Slow your life; it's not a race.
Find sweet healing at your own pace.

YOU CAN ONLY
SEE YOUR REFLECTION
IN STILL WATER.

Pearl started her journey down a path into the forest. She came to a meadow filled with beautiful flowers. When she stood still, she overheard a conversation between the bees buzzing nearby.

Just Bee

"What do you want to be?" asked the bee?

"I'm already a bee," answered the other bee.

The first bee glared. "No, when you grow up, what do you want to be?"

"Well, a bee, I suppose," said the second bee.

Very slowly the first bee said, "When you get bigger, what do you want to become?"

"Hmmmm," buzzed the bee. "Let me think about that."

Frustrated, the first bee said, "When you get older, what do you want to do?"

After a pause, the bee responded, "I suppose I will do what I'm already doing because I will still be me."

The first bee screamed, "Look, I don't think you understand how this works. Before you die, you must pick something to do or become."

"Why?" asked the bee.

"So you will have a purpose to your life. So you won't have lived for nothing. So you can be happy!"

The second bee nodded as if it understood but then said, "I think I'll just be."

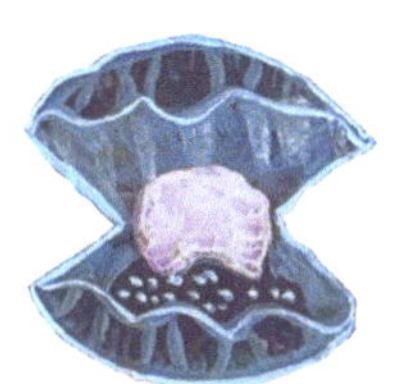

THE JOB OF SELF-CARE
IS A WORTHY CAREER.

From the far side of the meadow, a black rabbit hopped out in front of her, its large eyes filled with warning. "Beware of the traps laid by your own fears," it cautioned. "They will lure you away from your mission, if you let them."

Black Bunny

There was a black bunny that didn't have any friends,
same white, fuzzy nose and cottontail rear end.

But she was a loner and liked it like that,
no need for small talk in her large habitat.

Until one day she found a stranger,
one who presented no real danger.

He was a tall, old man with graying beard,
a magician who made things disappear.

"Oh, you'd be perfect as part of my show;
in the top hat, you'd hide, and no one would know.

"Would you like a job with lots of money?"
The rabbit thought this all seemed funny.

Pearl listened to the black bunny recount meeting the strangers in the forest.

Will he pay me in carrots or boatloads of greens?
Will my life get better than it already seems?

"I think not," the bunny replied as she hopped away.
Jobs are for suckers, she wanted to say.

The very next day, in the identical spot,
appeared a sexy iguana who liked her a lot.

"Shall we partner up and make lots of kids?"
the iguana tempted and batted its eyelids.

In one ear and out the other,
the rabbit didn't wish to become a mother.

"I think not," she started to say.
"Commitments are for suckers," she yelled as he slithered away.

She wondered what waited for her down the path as she cautiously exited
the meadow.

Left behind, sticking out of a crack
was some jagged glass that took her aback.

She had never seen a mirror before,
but she and black bunny had some kind of rapport.

Sure enough, the reflection stayed near;
as if in a dream, it whispered in her ear,

"I'm with you always. If you ever feel lonely,
just look into my eyes 'cause you're my one and only."

No commitments or jobs killing her vibe,
for that black bunny in the mirror was part of her tribe.

Pearl heard crying sounds that seemed to come from a well. She ran to look over the edge, but could only see her own reflection.

Pearl knew, despite feeling sad, she could embrace her purpose and continue to find wisdom. Her breath steadied as she realized she didn't have to be perfect. She just had to try. It was possible that by stepping through fear she would grow into the person she had always wanted to be, confident, brave, and true to herself.

From the Depths of Sadness

There once was a girl who lived in a well;
how she got there, no one could tell.
They say sadness was her middle name;
fear and self-loathing filled her with shame.

Surrounded by darkness, alone in the night,
she caught a glimpse of herself in the setting moonlight.
She shed a tear, first one and then many.
She cried for years, for her pain was plenty.

As all of her hopes floated away,
the floodgates opened, and they could hear her say:

I cry for my ancestors and all that they lost.
I cry for the villages, war-torn and squashed.
I cry for the witches, burned at the stake.
I cry for the girls who have been raped.
I cry for the victims and all of humanity.
I cry for straitjackets, bondage of insanity.
I cry for the person I will never become.
I cry for lost hopes, one by one.

She filled that well with all her tears,
her cries still heard after all these years.

DON'T IGNORE THE PAIN.
THAT'S THE GROWTH POINT.

Just beyond the well Pearl settled in a quiet place to sit under a tree and reflect on the past pain in her life. She realized that all her broken pieces had shaped her into the person she was becoming.

PEACE

Peace appears, not swirling wildly in the storm,
but where self-reflection and compassion start to take new form.

It doesn't arrive as a message floating by in the stream,
but when the water calms enough for crystal clarity.

It doesn't leave a map or use the GPS,
but sits alone among the groves of deeply rooted cypress.

Not found in the cyclone's storm or the debris,
but by mending a broken heart, one stitch, and then three.

And in that release of mourning the life not chosen,
it starts to beat again, healed heart now open.

Sun breaks through; regrets disappear,
that sound of a new life becoming absolutely clear.

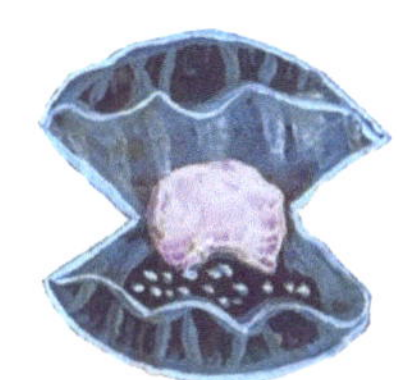

As Pearl walked farther, she came to a fork in the road, and for a moment, the path ahead seemed uncertain. She felt unsettled, her heart heavy with indecision. Hesitating, she feared she might choose wrongly and lose her way.

Perspective

I only see, from where I stand,
the world as it appears to me.
Empathy and compassion
may change my compass slightly.

But I cannot walk
in another's shoes,
no matter which
road I choose.

I can only paint
the world I see
from my experience
with the muse.

My job is to keep an open mind
to see beyond the veil.
Let imagination hold the brush.
That way, I cannot fail.

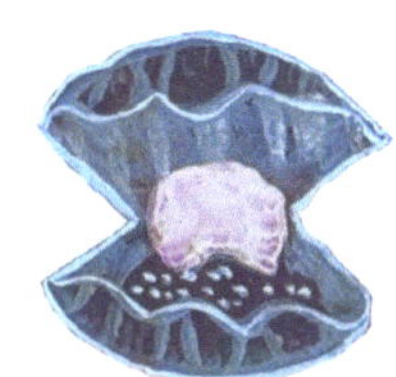

YOU MAY HAVE TO ALTER YOUR VIEW
TO SEE THE COMPLETE PICTURE.

Clutching the gifts from her journey so far, Pearl closed her eyes and took a deep breath, remembering the wisdom of her guides. She didn't need to know exactly where she was going. She just had to release her expectations. In that surrender, she found the freedom to continue walking. With each step, a new layer of her journey would be revealed.

SURRENDER

Ultimate pleasure awaits
in the release of expectations
when unattached to outcome,

in the space where there is no future.
Eyes open without distraction
when fiery core ignites and sparks fly

like contagious airborne particles.
Joy is shared with unsuspecting beings,
alive at last and truly living.

Feeling an embodied connection
with self and others,
peace only comes with complete surrender.

WHAT JOY AWAITS YOU
FROM LETTING GO?

At the top of the next ridge, Pearl found a bird in a cage. The bird's gaze met hers, and in that moment, she realized that she, too, was held back by her own fears. She decided to play a song, for the bird, on her horn.

Song of the Caged Bird

There was a bird that dreamed of flying free, but for as long as she could remember, she lived in a cage. Most of the time, she went about her day and forgot that she was caged. Somedays, if she closed one eye and got close enough to the edge, she could envision a life without bars.

She recalled a time when her mother told her about their ancestors. They were allowed to spread their wings, fly high, and soar through the sky. It sounded luxurious. That's what she dreamed of for herself.

Today, as she scratched through the food at the bottom of her cage, she found a piece of metal the size of a seed. It didn't taste good, so she left it alone. She noticed it was attached to another piece of metal. More and more bits of chain appeared until she realized they were all connected.

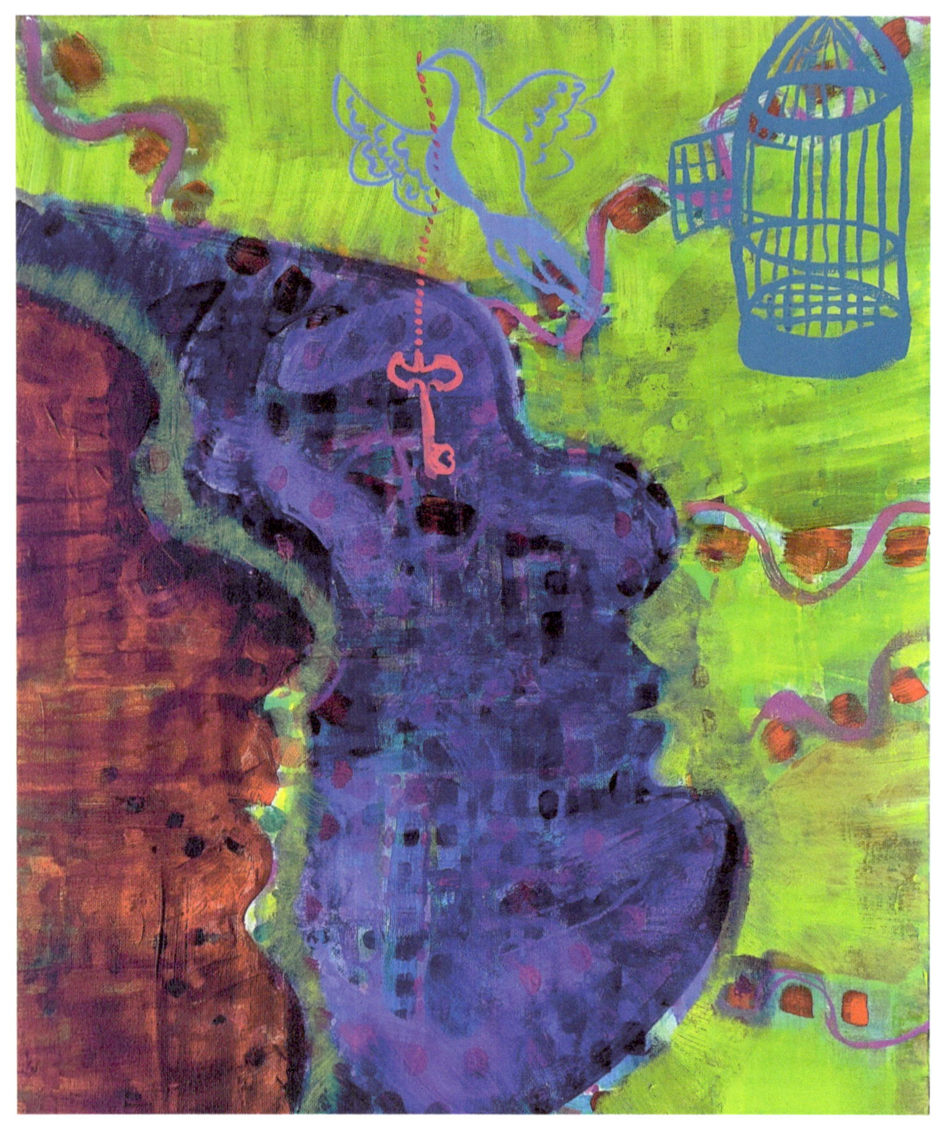

Pearl opened the cage door, releasing the bird from captivity, but it didn't fly away. She wondered why it stayed inside. Maybe the cage felt safe, the walls familiar, and the floor steady. The outside world, with all its vastness and unpredictability, was a place full of unknowns.

There was no pressure, no expectations, just the gentle pull of the world beyond. As Pearl stood there, she forgot her own fears and realized that freedom wasn't something that could be given. It was something she had to take for herself.

What a lovely golden chain, she thought. It was so pretty she wanted
to wear it. She tried to lift it and noticed a large key attached
to one end. She began to wonder if this key offered her some
sort of freedom.

She purposefully lifted the heavy key and unlocked
the door to the cage.

On the precipice of freedom, she felt paralyzed. Should she fly
away and explore the world and stretch her wings as her
ancestors had done? This is what she'd wanted for herself,
but caged life was all she had ever known and where
she felt most secure.

After the shock subsided, the bird knew she could no longer
pretend everything was unchanged. Life in the cage would never
be the same now that she had tasted freedom.
A better life was waiting for her when she was ready.

IT'S OKAY TO BE SCARED
AND FLY ANYWAY.

Pearl Meets All the Animals

"Who am I?" asked the ant.

All the other ants asked the same question
at the same time.

So loud was the question, as it echoed through the forest,
that it became "Who are we?"

The owls heard the question as if it were addressed to them
and answered, "Hoo, hoo, hoo."

The thunderous noise of all the world's ants asking, "Who are we?"
combined with all the talking owls saying, "Hoo, hoo, hoo,"
was so loud it woke the lioness. She found her voice and roared
to wake the rest of the pride, "Grrrr."

By now, all the insects and all the birds
and all the land animals had joined the inquiry.
"Grrrr." "Hoo, hoo." "Who are we?"

The whales deep in the ocean
knew something had changed
when they breached the surface
and spouted a mixture of air and water
before descending to the depths
to alert the other sea animals
through moaning songs
intertwined with high-pitched squeals.

To the core of the earth,
from the ocean floor,
the world slowly awakened
from a dormant state.

Volcanoes matched the whale's exhale.

The earth shook; the trees rattled; unsettled wings took flight.

The answer came from a voice above:

We are all one and the same.

Treat others with kindness.

For they are you, and you are Me.

We are all beings dressed in different skin, fur, and gills.

Look for the similarities, not differences.

Pearl looked up at the sky and gazed towards the sun on the horizon. She had traveled far, both in distance and in her heart. The paths she had walked had been winding and uncertain, filled with challenges and surprises, but she now felt a peaceful presence. Conscious of her ability to maneuver through pain, she embraced and radiated her confidence. She was ready to approach each sunrise, grateful for all her wisdom.

Come Play with Me

I am sadness and also joy;
I am fear and also excitement;
I am uncertainty and also knowing;
I am unearthed and also rooted;
I am shame and also buried;
I am growth and also blooming;
I am stillness and also serenity;
I am seeing and also visionary;
I am risk; come play with me.

REMEMBER TO
LIVE YOUR LIFE
IN FULL COLOR.

Let's Connect!

For more info visit: www.beezeecreates.com

Scan this QR code to view more of my paintings and hear my music.